FOREST HILLS, CA

2005

Forest Bootleg

NICOLE GOUX

atheneum NEW YORK LONDON TORONTO SYDNEY NEW DELHI

Hills Society

Dave Baker

SOMETHING
HORRIBLY VILE

AND EXTREMELY
REGRETTABLE

A BRIEF HISTORY OF KELLY'S OBSESSION WITH ANIME

KELLY FIRST DISCOVERED ANIME FROM HER COUSIN HAROLD, WHO WAS IN AN ANIME VHS TAPE TRADE-BY-MAIL GROUP. HER INITIAL EXPOSURE TOOK SHAPE IN THE FORM OF HIGHLY DEGRADED COPIES OF *BATTLE OF THE PLANETS/GATCHAMAN*. SHE DIDN'T INITIALLY CONNECT WITH THE MATERIAL.

HAD A DREAM LAST WEEK THAT SHE HAD DOG EARS LIKE INUYASHA

SECRETLY CONFUSED AS TO WHY HOT DOGS ARE CALLED HOT DOGS

KELLY, YOU DIDN'T LIKE THE WAY I WAS DRAWN?

WOULD "LITERALLY" DIE FOR A SET OF COMIC MARKERS

A FEW YEARS LATER SHE RAN ACROSS *METROPOLIS*. (NO, NOT THE GERMAN EXPRESSIONIST MOVIE, THE ANIME BY RINTARO AND KATSUHIRO OTOMO.) TO SAY IT SPARKED AN OBSESSION WOULD BE A GRAVE UNDERSTATEMENT.

SINCE THEN, SHE'S BEEN FEVERISHLY WATCHING AND COLLECTING ANIME. (NO, SHE DOESN'T LIKE MANGA THAT MUCH. IT'S TOO MUCH MONEY FOR HOW QUICKLY SHE READS THEM.)

YUKI PLUSH FROM *FRUITS BASKET* (BOUGHT WITH MOM'S CREDIT CARD)

CURRENTLY, SHE'S OBSESSED WITH *DRAGON BALL* AND HAYAO MIYAZAKI MOVIES.

SHE THINKS THE BURNED DVDs SHE'S JUST BOUGHT ARE *MY NEIGHBOR TOTORO* AND *PRINCESS MONONOKE*.

IS TOO BROKE TO BUY NEW UNDERWEAR

HATES PEANUT BUTTER

WHAT SHE DOESN'T KNOW IS THAT THEY'RE ACTUALLY...

BATTLE-DAMAGED *YU YU HAKUSHO* BOX SET FOUND AT A GARAGE SALE

A BRIEF HISTORY OF EVERY TIME BROOKE HAS THOUGHT ABOUT BURNING IN HELL

IT'S HOT!

BROOKE IMIFADON IS NOT FROM FOREST HILLS. SHE'S A PRODUCT OF SOUTHERN CALIFORNIA THROUGH AND THROUGH. THAT BEING SAID, HER UPBRINGING WASN'T THE AVERAGE CALIFORNIAN'S EXPERIENCE.

SOMEDAY I'LL HAVE FRIENDS

BROOKE'S FATHER, GABRIEL, WAS...WELL, THERE'S NO NICE WAY TO PUT THIS, SO WE'LL JUST COME OUT AND SAY IT. HE WAS IN A CULT. SO BROOKE WAS RAISED UNDER A VERY STRICT CHRISTIAN DOCTRINE. WHEN SHE TURNED FOURTEEN, SHE WAS TAKEN FROM HER FATHER'S CUSTODY AND GIVEN TO HER MOTHER...WHO *ALSO* HAS A VERY STRICT PERSONALITY.

BROOKE'S MOTHER, HAZEL JOHNSTON, IS AN INTELLECTUAL PROPERTY LAWYER. SHE'S A NO-NONSENSE WOMAN WHO AT TIMES SEEMS LIKE SHE ISN'T VERY HAPPY TO BE BROOKE'S MOTHER. TO SAY THEY HAVE A ROCKY RELATIONSHIP IS PUTTING IT LIGHTLY.

ARE YOU THERE, GOD? IT'S ME, BROOKE?

I HAVE SOME QUESTIONS ABOUT...

...EVERYTHING?

AFTER GOING THROUGH A ROUGH PATCH, BROOKE DECIDED SHE DIDN'T WANT TO GO TO PUBLIC SCHOOL. WHAT HAPPENED NEXT WAS NOT AT ALL WHAT BROOKE HAD ANTICIPATED. HER CONSERVATIVE CHRISTIAN GRANDMOTHER OFFERED TO PAY FOR HER TO ATTEND FOREST HILLS CHRISTIAN ACADEMY. A BOARDING SCHOOL FOR YOUNG PEOPLE...*OF FAITH*.

HAZEL DECIDED BROOKE WOULD ATTEND. IT WOULD PROVIDE HER WITH STRUCTURE AND BRING HER CLOSER TO GOD.

HAS ANY OF THAT HAPPENED?

WELL, SHE'S SITTING ON A COUCH WATCHING A SEVENTY-FOOT-TALL METAL WOMAN FIRE LASERS OUT OF HER BREASTS TO SAVE A CITY FROM BIZARRELY PHALLIC-LOOKING SQUID MONSTERS...

SO...

YOU BE THE JUDGE.

BROOKE'S SIN BINGO

I LOVE YOU, KELLY.

A BRIEF HISTORY OF BROOKE'S LONELINESS

BROOKE HAS KNOWN SHE WAS A LESBIAN SINCE SHE WAS 7 AND 4/7 YEARS OLD. SHE WAS SITTING IN CHURCH WITH HER FATHER WHEN THE REALIZATION CAME. SHE COULDN'T TAKE HER EYES OFF OF MRS. CHATTERJEE. SHE WAS THE MOST BEAUTIFUL WOMAN BROOKE HAD EVER SEEN.

BROOKE DIDN'T EVEN HAVE A CONCEPT OF SEXUAL IDENTITY YET, BUT SHE KNEW DEEP IN HER BONES THAT SHE WANTED TO BE AS CLOSE TO MRS. CHATTERJEE AS SHE COULD. SHE ALSO FELT VERY ALONE IN THIS MOMENT, BECAUSE SHE UNDERSTOOD THAT MRS. CHATTERJEE WOULD NEVER FEEL THE SAME WAY ABOUT HER.

ON HER NINTH BIRTHDAY, BROOKE WANTED A PAIR OF OVERALLS. HER FATHER SAID NO, BECAUSE PANTS WERE MEANT FOR MEN. SHE DIDN'T KNOW HOW TO PARSE THIS AT THE TIME, BUT SHE KNEW THAT HER FATHER'S WORDS HAD A MEANING SHE WAS NOT FULLY GRASPING.

THEY WOULDN'T SPEAK OF THIS AGAIN UNTIL BROOK WAS THIRTEEN, WHEN HER DAD FOUND A FOLDER UNDER HER BED FILLED WITH MAGAZINE CUTOUTS OF SWIMSUIT MODELS. SHE TRIED TO EXPLAIN, BUT BEFORE SHE COULD FINISH...HE BURST INTO TEARS AND LEFT THE ROOM.

THIS WAS THE ONLY TIME SHE'D EVER SEE HIM CRY.

BROOKE TRIED TO CONVINCE HERSELF SHE WASN'T GAY AFTER THAT. SHE PERFORMATIVELY TALKED ABOUT BOYS IN FRONT OF HER FATHER. THIS WORKED ABOUT AS WELL AS YOU'D EXPECT.

AND THEN, BEFORE SHE KNEW IT...SHE WAS LIVING WITH HER MOM...AND LIFE WAS VERY DIFFERENT, IN BOTH GOOD AND BAD WAYS.

WHEN BROOKE WAS FIRST KISSED BY HENRY VICENTE OUTSIDE THE REC CENTER FOUR SUMMERS AGO, IT WAS EMPTY AND BIZARRELY WET. LIKE HE JUST LICKED HER FACE. SHE DID NOT FEEL ANY HUMAN CONNECTION IN THAT MOMENT.

TO SAY THAT A PERVADING FEELING OF ISOLATION HAS BEEN THE ONE CONSTANT IN BROOKE'S LIFE WOULD BE PRETTY ACCURATE.

AND THIS MOMENT. RIGHT NOW. DESPITE DATING KELLY FOR OVER FOUR MONTHS AND BEING FRIENDS WITH HER FOR WHO-KNOWS-HOW-LONG AND LOVING HER MORE THAN LIFE ITSELF... BROOKE FEELS AS THOUGH HER PHYSICAL PRESENCE ON EARTH MATTERS TO A GRAND TOTAL OF ZERO PEOPLE.

BUT ALSO PIZZA IS PRETTY COOL, SO, WHAT-THE-F@*K-EVER.

Chapter: 2

THE
WILLING
&
THE
ABLE

MAN, IT'S SO QUIET IN HERE.

ERIKA HOLLINGS'S BED

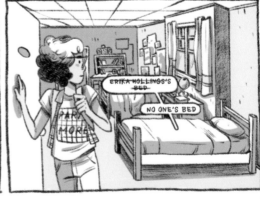

ERIKA HOLLINGS'S BED

NO ONE'S BED

ERIKA HOLLINGS WAS BROOKE'S ROOMMATE. SHE COMMITTED SUICIDE IN THE GYM SHOWERS, STILL IN HER CLOTHES. BROOKE DOESN'T LIKE TO TALK ABOUT IT.

ERIKA WAS A QUARRELSOME PERSON WHO COULD HAVE FOUND A REASON TO PICK A FIGHT WITH ANYONE.

BROOKE LIKED THIS ABOUT HER. SHE ENJOYED THE BACK-AND-FORTH.

MOST OF THE TIME.

THE WEIRDEST PART IS HOW QUICKLY EVERYONE HAS MOVED ON. YES, IT WAS AT THE BEGINNING OF THE YEAR, BUT IT'S ALMOST LIKE IT NEVER HAPPENED.

EXCEPT THERE'S AN EMPTY BED IN BROOKE'S ROOM.

ALL THE PEOPLE WHO DIDN'T KNOW ERIKA PRETENDED THAT SHE MEANT SO MUCH TO THEM...

ALL THE TEACHERS CHECKED IN ON BROOKE, AS IF SHE HAD BEEN ERIKA'S FAMILY...

THEY WERE ROOMMATES FOR SIX WEEKS.

BROOKE STILL DOESN'T KNOW WHY ERIKA KILLED HERSELF.

ALL SHE DOES KNOW IS THAT SHE'S GLAD THE GRIEF COUNSELORS AND FORCED MOURNING ARE OVER.

TO COMPOUND THINGS, MRS. GRAHAM, THE LIVE-IN DORMS SUPERVISOR, DIED TWO MONTHS AGO.

FOREST HILLS CHRISTIAN ACADEMY IS STILL SEARCHING FOR A REPLACEMENT...

IF YOU'RE A WOMAN OF FAITH WHO HAS TWO TO FIVE YEARS' EXPERIENCE WORKING WITH TEENAGERS AND WANT FREE ROOM AND BOARD ON TOP OF A TEACHER'S SALARY... APPLICATIONS ARE WELCOME.

FOREST HILLS, CA

POPULATION 9,003

FOUNDED IN 1881

A MINING TOWN UNTIL THE 1970S, FOREST HILLS WAS REBORN WHEN THE CHRISTIAN BOARDING SCHOOL WAS NEWLY ESTABLISHED.

IT'S FAIR TO SAY THAT FOREST HILLS EXISTS TO SERVICE THE SCHOOL. THE ONLY OTHER HIGH SCHOOL IN THE AREA, GEORGE EL CAMINO HIGH, IS A SEVEN-TOWN SCHOOL.

THE MOST EXCITING THING THAT HAPPENS IN FOREST HILLS IS WHEN THE ACADEMY FOOTBALL TEAM PLAYS THE EL CAMINO HIGH FOOTBALL TEAM.

LAST YEAR, WILLIE LOOMIS'S COUSIN BEN GOT TACKLED SO HARD HE S#!T HIS PANTS. OBVIOUSLY, HE MOVED SCHOOL DISTRICTS IMMEDIATELY.

FOREST HILLS COULD BE DESCRIBED AS A "SMALL TOWN," WHICH IS TRUE, BUT DOESN'T BEGIN TO EXAMINE THE DEPTHS OF THE REPRESSIVE AND TOXIC CULTURE IT PRODUCES, DESPITE HAVING RECENTLY ENTERED THE NEW MILLENNIUM.

BROOKE AND HER FRIENDS ARE CONSISTENTLY REFERRED TO AS "THOSE GIRLS" WITH A KNOWING TONE. SO, Y'KNOW, *THAT'S FUN.*

SO?

YA, IT'S COOL.

HAVE YOU MADE IT TO THAT SUPERLOVE EPISODE WITH THE GIGANTIC BAT CREATURES?

THAT S#!T IS SO CRAZY. WHOEVER MADE THOSE DESIGNS... MAN...ON ANOTHER LEVEL...

LIKE SERIOUSLY? CAN YOU BELIEVE A HUMAN CAME UP WITH THAT?

YOU HAVEN'T MADE IT THERE, HAVE YOU?

NO, NOT YET.

YOU HAVE TO...

YOU JUST HAVE TO, REALLY.

...

YEAH, I'LL DEFINITELY DO THAT.

BUMP

A BRIEF HISTORY OF THE SMALL LIFE OF MAGGIE HILCOT

MAGGIE HILCOT WAS BORN AND RAISED IN FOREST HILLS. SURPRISINGLY, SHE LIKES IT.

MAGGIE ISN'T REALLY THE TYPE WHO HAS A WIDE SOCIAL CIRCLE. MOST OF HER ACQUAINTANCES ARE EITHER FROM CHURCH OR FROM THAT MAGICAL THING THAT HAPPENS IN SMALL TOWNS WHERE...EVERYONE JUST SEEMS TO KNOW ONE ANOTHER.

MAGGIE BELIEVES DEEPLY THAT THE LORD IS WATCHING OVER HER AND HER MOTHER. EVER SINCE HER FATHER LEFT WHEN SHE WAS SIX, SHE'S FELT A DIVINE SPIRIT GUIDING HER PATH, KEEPING HER FROM HARM.

MAGGIE'S A RARE BIRD IN THAT HER DREAMS ARE QUIET: HAVING REAL FRIENDSHIPS, EVENTUALLY KISSING A BOY, AND HELPING HER MOTHER PAY OFF THEIR HOUSE.

MAGGIE MET THE FOREST HILLS GIRLS IN A VERY HUMOROUS AND HAPHAZARD WAY...BUT THAT'S A STORY FOR LATER...

A BRIEF HISTORY OF MELISSA CHO'S LEFT SOCK

MELISSA'S FAMILY MOVED AROUND A LOT WHEN SHE WAS LITTLE. AND WHEN WE SAY "MELISSA'S FAMILY," WE LITERALLY MEAN HER WHOLE FAMILY. HER GRANDPARENTS, HER FATHER, MOTHER, AND OLDER BROTHER MOVED FOUR TIMES BETWEEN WHEN MELISSA WAS FOUR TO ELEVEN.

MELISSA'S MOTHER, JOAN, IS THE BREADWINNER IN THE FAMILY. SHE WORKS IN THE HIGH-STAKES WORLD OF PAPER CLIP MANUFACTURING. JOAN IS A BRIGHT WOMAN WHO OVERSEES MANUFACTURING PLANT REHABILITATIONS.

MELISSA NEVER REALLY BONDED WITH HER MOTHER OVER ANY COMMON INTERESTS. SHE SPENT MOST OF HER TIME ALONE, OR WITH HER GRANDFATHER, WHO DIDN'T TALK MUCH. HOWEVER, ON HER THIRTEENTH BIRTHDAY, HE GIFTED MELISSA WITH A PAIR OF CIRCUS-BRANDED SOCKS. MOST GIRLS HER AGE WOULD HAVE THOUGHT THEY WERE FOR LITTLE KIDS, BUT MELISSA'S LOVE OF THE TRAPEZE TRIUMPHED. SHE STILL HAS THEM TO THIS DAY.

WELL, ONE OF THEM, ANYWAY...

SHE'S CURRENTLY WEARING IT...

...ON HER LEFT FOOT.

YOU READY?

YEAH, RIGHT BEHIND YOU.

A BRIEF HISTORY OF MELISSA CHO'S MUSTACHE

MELISSA'S FAMILY MOVED FROM EUGENE, OREGON, TO OAKLAND, CALIFORNIA, WHEN SHE WAS ELEVEN YEARS OLD.

SOON AFTER THAT, SHE NOTICED PEACH FUZZ GROWING ON HER UPPER LIP.

SHE'S BEEN TWEEZING IT FOR THE PAST FIVE YEARS. EVERY OTHER WEEK SHE PRAYS TO GOD, ASKING WHY HE HAS INFLICTED THIS ON HER.

EVERY OTHER WEDNESDAY, SHE DEBATES SHAVING IT. BUT SHE HEARD THAT IF YOU SHAVE HAIR, IT WILL COME BACK THICKER...AND SHE'S PRETTY SURE SHE DOESN'T WANT A FULL BEARD.

IF SHE HAD A BEARD, SHE'D PROBABLY RUN AWAY.

OR JOIN THE CIRCUS.

MAYBE LIFE WITH A BEARD WOULD BE WAY BETTER.

IT'S JUST THIS MIDDLE-GROUND MUSTACHE LIFE THAT IS SO DEPRESSING.

SINCE SHE WAS ENROLLED AT FOREST HILLS BY HER MOTHER, TWEEZING HAS BEEN SLIGHTLY MORE DIFFICULT. SHE'S FOUND THAT DOING IT IN BETWEEN SECOND AND THIRD PERIOD IS THE BEST OPTION. OR LATE AT NIGHT. BUT WHO WANTS TO LOSE SLEEP?

THAT S#!T SUCKS.

Chapter: 3

A BRIEF HISTORY OF KELLY'S COMPLEX RELATIONSHIP WITH CHRISTIANITY †

KELLY WAS RAISED AS A CHRISTIAN. A METHODIST, TO BE EXACT. WHEN HER PATERNAL GRANDPARENTS IMMIGRATED FROM SAUDI ARABIA, THEY BEFRIENDED A GROUP OF METHODISTS IN NORTH DAKOTA. HER FATHER BECAME DEEPLY INVOLVED IN THE CHURCH AND PASSED THAT ON TO KELLY. IT WAS GOOD SOMETIMES...AND NOT GOOD OTHER TIMES.

ATTENDING FOREST HILLS HAS BEEN GOOD FOR KELLY BECAUSE IT'S NON-DENOMINATIONAL. IT'S ALLOWED HER A BIT MORE ELASTICITY THAN SHE PREVIOUSLY WAS ALLOWED IN HER FATHER'S STRICT HOUSEHOLD.

THESE DAYS KELLY TRIES NOT TO THINK ABOUT GOD. AS MUCH AS YOU CAN IN A SCHOOL THAT'S ALL ABOUT...WELL, GOD. OCCASIONALLY, SHE STILL GETS PANGS OF GUILT FOR SWEARING, KISSING BROOKE, AND EVEN...WATCHING ANIME.

THE BIGGEST TURNING POINT FOR KELLY WAS WHEN SHE FIRST KISSED HELEN MACGUIRE IN EIGHTH GRADE...AND THE WORLD DIDN'T END.

THERE'S STILL A DARK NIGHT OR TWO WHERE SHE PRAYS TO THE BIG G, BUT THE ONE THING SHE'S CERTAIN IS THAT HE, SHE, OR IT DOESN'T GIVE TWO S#!TS IF SHE HAS PREMARITAL SEX.

ALSO: SHE WANTS TO HOG ALL THE ANIME FOR HERSELF...*JUST A LITTLE.*

IF YOU'RE GONNA LIVE LIFE TOO SCARED OF GETTING CAUGHT TO TAKE RISKS, YOU'LL NEVER GET ANY COOL JACKETS, METAPHORICAL OR OTHERWISE.

OKAY.

FINE.

MAYBE JUST THIS ONCE.

WE GOT ONE BITE. WHY ARE NONE OF THESE OTHER DUDES INTO IT?

WHAT ARE YOU GIRLS TALKING ABOUT?

NOTHING, MOM.

GO STRAIGHT HOME AFTER. DON'T--

MOM.

YOU'RE DROPPING US OFF AT YOUTH GROUP...

ALL RIGHT, HAVE FUN, GIRLS.

I LOVE YOU, MAGGIE... AND WE'RE HERE FOR YOU...BUT I CAN'T BELIEVE WE'RE DOING THIS AGAIN.

LAST TIME WE WERE HERE, SOME DUDE COUGHED IN MY MOUTH WHILE WE WERE SINGING "I COULD SING OF YOUR LOVE FOREVER."

HE DID NOT... YOUR MOUTH JUST KINDA GOT IN HIS BLAST RADIUS.

THINK ABOUT WHAT YOU JUST SAID TO ME RIGHT NOW.

I KINDA LIKE YOUTH GROUP.

WELL, THAT WAS THE LAST THING I EXPECTED YOU TO SAY.

AT LEAST I KNOW ONE OF US BESIDES ME HAS GOOD TASTE, THEN.

C'MON, LET'S GO WORSHIP.

I DON'T KNOW WHAT'S MORE ANNOYING: MELISSA INEXPLICABLY LIKING THIS BULLS#!t...

...OR MAGGIE... JUST BEING MAGGIE.

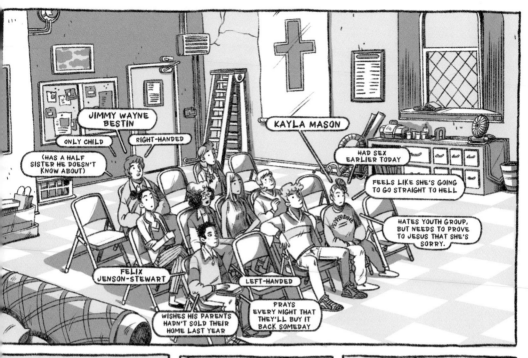

JIMMY WAYNE BESTIN

ONLY CHILD

RIGHT-HANDED

(HAS A HALF SISTER HE DOESN'T KNOW ABOUT)

KAYLA MASON

HAD SEX EARLIER TODAY

FEELS LIKE SHE'S GOING TO GO STRAIGHT TO HELL

HATES YOUTH GROUP, BUT NEEDS TO PROVE TO JESUS THAT SHE'S SORRY.

FELIX JENSON-STEWART

LEFT-HANDED

WISHES HIS PARENTS HADN'T SOLD THEIR HOME LAST YEAR

PRAYS EVERY NIGHT THAT THEY'LL BUY IT BACK SOMEDAY

OH MAN, I'M SO EXHAUSTED FROM MY GOSH-DANG JOB. THIS JOB IN AN OFFICE BUILDING WHERE I CLEAN THE FLOORS AT NIGHT.

OH GOD.

I FORGOT HE DOES THIS.

HOW COULD YOU?

I PRAY AT NIGHT THAT THE LORD WILL HELP ME OUT OF THIS SITUATION. THAT HE'LL HELP ME CLEAN MY SOUL.

I JUST NEED TO KEEP THE FAITH AND PUT ONE FOOT IN FRONT OF THE OTHER...

BECAUSE WHAT I DON'T REALIZE IS THAT EVEN THOUGH IT LOOKS LIKE I'VE PAINTED MYSELF INTO A CORNER...

...THE LORD IS ACTUALLY HELPING ME PAINT A MOSAIC THAT WILL BE SEEN BY EVERYONE AS A TESTAMENT TO MY FAITH.

WHY IS HE TALKING ABOUT PAINTING WHILE HE'S HOLDING A MOP? IS THE MOP SUPPOSED TO BE A PAINT BRUSH? IS HE PRETENDING TO PAINT THE FLOOR? IS THE FLOOR ACTUALLY A WALL?

I FEEL LIKE EVERY OTHER THING YOU SAID WOULD MAKE A GOOD ANIME TITLE.

AN ANIME ABOUT PAINTING THE WALLS OF A CHURCH? THAT SOUNDS AWFUL.

...

I'D WATCH IT...

AS LONG AS THERE WAS A LOVE TRIANGLE.

LIFE CAN APPEAR AS A SERIES OF CLOSED DOORS, TO SOMEONE WHO REFUSES TO SEE.

THE MIXED METAPHORS HERE ARE GOING TO GIVE ME AN ANEURYSM.

BROOKE.

LOOK AT HIM...

THE MAN THINKS FROSTED TIPS AREN'T JUST A GOOD CHOICE... BUT A GREAT ONE.

I'VE NEVER SEEN ANYONE FROST THAT HARD.

I CAN HONESTLY SAY THAT I AGREE.

THAT MAN FROSTS.

THE HARDEST.

AND THAT, MY YOUNG FRIENDS, IS WHY IT'S IMPORTANT TO SEE CLEARLY AND LIVE TRUTHFULLY...

...WITH THE LORD IN YOUR HEART.

OKAY, BUT ENOUGH ABOUT ME...

THIS IS EXTREME CHRIST LOVE YOUTH GROUP. WE'RE HERE TO LOVE TOGETHER.

C'MON NOW, EVERYONE.

JASON LANSING

HAS BEEN RUNNING THIS YOUTH GROUP SINCE HIS SISTER MOVED TO UTAH WITH A GUY NAMED TED

LET'S SING.

OWNS FOUR PAIRS OF BOARD SHORTS

THREE PUKA-SHELL NECKLACES

PEOPLE NAMED TED DON'T GET MARRIED

HAS ONE HANDMADE JESUS FISH LEATHER WRISTBAND

RIGHT-HANDED

IS CONSIDERING GOING BACK TO SCHOOL FOR ELECTRICAL ENGINEERING

HAS BEEN INTERNALLY DEBATING GETTING A CHAIN FOR HIS WALLET

DOES INDEED FROST HARD

YEAH... TOTALLY.

YEAH, I KNEW YOU'D TOTALLY GET IT.

BECAUSE YOU REALLY UNDERSTAND. YOU TALK TO GOD OFTEN, DON'T YOU, BREANNA.

MY NAME IS... BROOKE?

YEAH, RIGHT. SORRY. BROOKE AND BREANNA ARE JUST SIMILAR.

I GOT THEM BACKWARD.

~~KELLY~~

BREANNA

YEAH, IT HAPPENS TO US ALL THE TIME.

WELL, WE'RE GONNA WALK HOME NOW.

JUST...MAKE SURE YOU GUYS ARE REALLY WALKING WITH THE LORD.

IT'S IMPORTANT, NOW MORE THAN EVER.

WE ALWAYS WALK WITH THE LORD, MR. JASON.

NIGHT, GIRLS.

THAT DUDE IS THE LIVING EMBODIMENT OF FROST HARD.

HE'S SO FROSTED, YOU DON'T EVEN NEED TO SAY "HARD." IT, QUITE LITERALLY, GOES WITHOUT SAYING.

KELLY FEELS CLOSER TO BROOKE RIGHT NOW THAN SHE HAS IN A LONG TIME.

SHE WANTS TO SAY "I LOVE YOU" RIGHT NOW...

BUT THE TIMING... JUST ISN'T RIGHT.

WHICH WILL BE A CONSTANT FEELING, FOR THE REST OF KELLY'S LIFE.

I STILL CAN'T BELIEVE WE DIDN'T SELL MORE DVDs. WELL, I GUESS THAT'S HOW OUR GRAND EXPERIMENT ENDS.

IT WAS AS NOBLE AS IT WAS TENTACLE LADEN.

I WOULD SAY WE GAVE IT OUR BEST SHOT, BUT I REALLY DIDN'T.

AND YOU'RE THE ONLY ONE OUT OF US WHO SOLD ANYTHING.

I WONDER HOW MAGGIE IS DOING.

HEY, WHAT'S THAT?

NOTHING.

C'MON, WHAT IS IT?

SHOW ME.

HEY, MELISSA...

YEAH?

UM... ...CAN I TALK TO YOU FOR A SECOND?

IS THIS WHAT I THINK IT IS?

IT WOULD APPEAR SO?

ARE WE ABOUT TO BE RICH? ARE WE ABOUT TO BUY F@*KING JACKETS? AND ALL THE SHIVER ME BURGERS WE CAN EAT?

I THINK SO?

WELL, THAT WAS, LIKE, UNEXPECTED.

WHAT HAPPENED?

WELL--

MR. PENDERGAST

CHEMISTRY TEACHER

WANTED TO BE A CROSS-COUNTRY RUNNER

STILL MIGHT DO IT...

SOMEDAY

LADIES? ARE WE PLANNING TO ENTER THE CLASSROOM?

YES, MR. PENDERGAST.

MAN, I HATE IT WHEN YOU GUYS DO THAT.

SO, WHAT HAPPENS NEXT?

THAT'S A VERY GOOD QUESTION...

A BRIEF HISTORY OF MAGGIE'S UNFULFILLED DESIRES

ALL MAGGIE WANTS IN THE WORLD IS TO BE ENROLLED AT FOREST HILLS CHRISTIAN ACADEMY. SHE'S BEEN BEGGING HER MOM TO SEND HER THERE FOR THE LAST YEAR AND A HALF, BUT THE TUITION IS JUST TOO EXPENSIVE. CAROL'S CONSTANT REFRAIN IS "WHY WOULD I SEND YOU TO A BOARDING SCHOOL THAT'S IN THE SAME TOWN WE LIVE IN?"

MAGGIE NEVER HAS A GOOD ANSWER FOR THAT QUESTION. SHE DOESN'T HAVE THE WORDS TO COMMUNICATE THE SENSE OF BELONGING AND STRENGTH SHE FINDS IN HER FRIENDS. SHE STUMBLES WHEN TRYING TO RELAY THAT THE SCHOOL IS BETTER SUITED FOR HER BECAUSE IT WILL DEEPEN HER CONNECTION WITH GOD.

EVERY TIME THEY HAVE THIS CONVERSATION, CAROL KNOWS HOW TO POKE HOLES IN MAGGIE'S ARGUMENTS. "WHEN YOU WERE IN FIFTH GRADE AND BECKY WILLIAMS GOT BRACES, YOU WANTED BRACES." "TWO SUMMERS AGO, YOU TRIED OUT FOR SWIM TEAM BECAUSE YOU WENT TO A SLEEPOVER AT MEGAN HITCHENS'S HOUSE, AND THEY HAD A POOL."

SOMETIMES MAGGIE SITS ALONE AT NIGHT AND FEELS EMPTY. NOT LONELY OR DEPRESSED, JUST EMPTY. LIKE A BARREN WASTELAND OF ABSENCE AND WANT.

MAGGIE KNOWS THAT HER MOTHER THINKS SHE'S COMFORTABLE IN THE ROLE OF A FOLLOWER. MAGGIE KNOWS THAT HER MOTHER DOESN'T LIKE THIS BECAUSE IT REMINDS HER OF THE WORST PARTS OF HERSELF.

AND, YES...ON A BAD DAY, MAGGIE IS COMFORTABLE AS A FOLLOWER. BUT ULTIMATELY, SHE'S JUST LOOKING FOR SOMETHING TO HELP HER THROUGH THE DAY...BESIDES HER FAITH. BECAUSE AS MUCH AS SHE HESITATES TO ADMIT IT...SOMETIMES, FAITH ISN'T ENOUGH FOR MAGGIE.

I JUST CAN'T BELIEVE THIS IS WORKING.

I'VE ALWAYS TOLD YOU THAT ANIME IS THE BEST.

MAYBE NOW YOU'LL WATCH MORE WITH ME.

YEAH, YOU'RE RIGHT. ALSO: ONE OF THE BOYS WAS TELLING ME ABOUT THIS WEIRD SERIES CALLED FULLMETAL ALCHEMIST, AND IT SOUNDS COOL.

HA! YOU'VE ADMITTED I'M RIGHT ABOUT SOMETHING!

ALL HAIL THE OMNISCIENT POWERS OF ANIME!

DO YOU GUYS WANT TO SPEND THE NIGHT AT MY PLACE TONIGHT? WE CAN PLAN--

I DON'T KNOW.

WE SHOULD PROBABLY KEEP A LOW PROFILE WHILE ALL THIS STUFF IS HAPPENING.

MELISSA AND I ALMOST GOT CAUGHT TWO TIMES AGO WHEN WE WERE SNEAKING BACK IN THE MORNING.

YEAH, TODAY HAS BEEN A REALLY GOOD DAY. LET'S NOT PUSH IT.

OKAY, WELL, TOMORROW AFTER SCHOOL, THEN? SHIVER ME BURGERS?

COOL. SOUNDS GOOD TO ME.

YEAH.

YEP.

OH, THANKS.

A BRIEF HISTORY OF KELLY'S TRAUMA

KELLY NAHAS HAS NEVER REALLY FELT LIKE SHE FIT IN. SHE'S ALWAYS BEEN SET APART, EITHER BY HER INTERESTS OR HOW SHE ACTS.

inSULT BINGO

B!*CH	C$#T	F@*KFACE	D*%E	F$#@!T
23x	3x	4x	17x	1x
T@#$L HEAD[1]	S#!TFACE	★	RUG MUNCHER	C$M GUZZLER[2]
1x	2x		3x	1x
IDIOT	A#$HOLE	H@%$I[3]	F@*K-SL#T	S!@G[4]
43x	22x	3x	2x	6x

1 T@#$L HEAD – OUTSIDE OF A CONVENIENCE STORE, A SMALL BLONDE BOY MUMBLED THIS SLUR AT KELLY. SHE'S NEVER FORGOTTEN HIS FACE.

2 C$M GUZZLER– AN OLD MAN SCREAMED THIS AT KELLY WHILE SHE WAS WALKING TO HER BEST FRIEND'S HOUSE IN SECOND GRADE.

3 H@%$I – TWO OLDER GIRLS KEPT REFERRING TO KELLY BY THIS WHEN SHE FIRST GOT TO FOREST HILLS. SHE THOUGHT IT WAS A NICKNAME, UNTIL ONE OF THE TEACHERS REPRIMANDED THE OLDER GIRLS.

4 KELLY'S STILL NOT SURE WHAT THE NAME IS IN REFERENCE TO. SOMETHING ABOUT A CARTOON? LIKE NOT AN ANIME?

ALL THESE TRANSGRESSIONS PALE IN COMPARISON TO BECKY McLEAN'S SIXTH-GRADE BIRTHDAY PARTY.

AFTER A RAUCOUS DAY OF FUN AND PRESENTS, SOMEONE SUGGESTED THE GIRLS PLAY TWISTER, A SEEMINGLY INNOCENT WAY TO SPEND THE EVENING.

HOWEVER, DURING THE GAME, ARI SHERMAN'S HEAD ENDED UP FRIGHTENINGLY CLOSE TO KELLY'S CROTCH. THIS WAS A TAD TOO MUCH FOR KELLY'S NEWLY BURGEONING HORMONES TO HANDLE...

...AND SHE BEGAN TO GET TURNED ON.

ABRUPTLY, ARI STOPPED PLAYING THE GAME AND SAID SHE COULD HEAR KELLY GETTING WET. ALL THE GIRLS BEGAN TO HOWL WITH LAUGHTER, HUMILIATING KELLY. SHE WAS CRUSHED.

KELLY PHONED HER MOM AND WAS PROMPTLY PICKED UP FROM THE WOULD-BE SLEEPOVER. KELLY DIDN'T SAY ANYTHING FOR THE DURATION OF THE RIDE HOME.

SHE'S STILL NEVER TOLD ANYONE ABOUT WHAT HAPPENED AT BECKY McLEAN'S SIXTH-GRADE PARTY...

YEAH, YOU'RE RIGHT.

I'LL TRY TO... BE MORE RELAXED.

WHAT?

HOLD THE PHONE! HOLD THE PHONE!

EVERYBODY STOP DOING WHAT YOU'RE DOING!

WHAT?

WHAT ARE YOU GUYS FREAKING OUT ABOUT?

MAGGIE.

ARE YOU OKAY?

ARE YOU ALL RIGHT?

YOU'RE NOT ACTING LIKE YOURSELF.

I'M FINE.

I'M JUST... TRYING TO HELP US MAKE THIS THING WORK.

WOW.

I FEEL LIKE WE'RE REALLY COMING TOGETHER...WE SHOULD, LIKE, HAVE A NAME. LIKE, IF WE WERE AN ANIME, WHAT WOULD OUR ANIME BE CALLED?

DO YOU THINK THEY GET TIRED OF SAYING "ARRRGH, MATEYS. WELCOME TO SHIVER ME BURGERS. WHAT CAN I GET STARTED FOR YE LAND LUBBERS?"

YES, OBVIOUSLY.

THERE'S ALMOST, LIKE, A MONASTIC QUALITY TO IT, THOUGH. I WOULD ENJOY SAYING IT REPEATEDLY. IT'S ALMOST MUSICAL. LIKE A MANTRA.

WELL, MOST HUMANS WOULDN'T.

DO YOU THINK THEY GET FREE FOOD?

THEY HAVE TO, RIGHT?

THAT'S GOT TO BE, LIKE, THE ONLY PERK OF WORKING HERE.

A BRIEF HISTORY OF A TEXTILES MANUFACTURING PLANT

EVER SINCE TEEN HEARTTHROB GEORGIO SIMONE WAS SPOTTED ON THE RED CARPET SPORTING A MERZO SPEED FREAK DOWN JACKET TWO NEW YORK FASHION WEEKS AGO, YOUNG PEOPLE ACROSS THE COUNTRY HAVE BEEN CLAMORING FOR THE GARMENT TO BE AVAILABLE COMMERCIALLY.

HOWEVER, THE $529.99 RETAIL PRICE WAS A RED FLAG FOR MOST U.S.-BASED RETAIL-CHAIN BUYERS. THUS, THE COMPANY MERZO FASHION LLC. STEPPED UP TO THE CHALLENGE.

WITH THEIR NEW MANUFACTURING PLANT OVERSEAS, THEY'VE BEEN PRODUCING NEARLY IDENTICAL JACKETS FOR A QUARTER OF THE RETAIL PRICE. BIG BOX RETAIL CHAINS ACROSS THE COUNTRY HAVE BEEN SUPPLYING MERZO HEADQUARTERS WITH ORDERS BY THE DUMP-TRUCK LOAD.

MOST PEOPLE DON'T KNOW THAT THEIR NEW JACKETS ARE PRODUCED BY WORKERS PAID CENTS ON THE DOLLAR, THAT THEY'RE FORCED TO ENDURE GRUELING SCHEDULES, AND THAT FOUR FACTORY WORKERS PASSED AWAY LAST WINTER FROM A GAS LEAK.

THEY ONLY CARE ABOUT THE JACKETS, WELL...BECAUSE THEY JUST LOOK COOL.

KIMMIE BRINKLEY

JANESSA'S BEST FRIEND

SECOND MOST POPULAR GIRL IN SCHOOL

ALSO HAS THE COOL JACKET

LEFT-HANDED

HAD SEX WITH CHAD BEYERS UNDER THE BLEACHERS LAST YEAR

IT WAS UNDERWHELMING

HEY...

HEY...

SO... ...I HEARD FROM EDDIE WHAT YOU'VE BEEN DOING...

WE HAVE NO IDEA WHAT YOU'RE TALKING ABOUT...

SURE. WHATEVER.

I MEAN IT'S NERD S#!T...

BUT STILL... IT'S PRETTY COOL OR WHATEVER...

WE NEED TO GET OUT OF HERE IMMEDIATELY.

WE HAVE TO TALK ABOUT THIS.

NOW.

LOOK AT US... DO YOU REALLY THINK WE'RE EVER GOING TO BE ON JANESSA'S LEVEL?

SPEAK FOR YOURSELF. JANESSA IS TRYING TO GET ON MY LEVEL.

IS SHE, THOUGH?

WELL, LOOK. WE CAN'T REALLY DO ANYTHING RIGHT NOW, ANYWAY.

WE NEED TO SET UP A RESUPPLY RUN.

WE NEED MORE INVENTORY BEFORE WE DECIDE WHAT TO DO WITH OUR WAR CHEST.

THE ECSTASY OF BEING MISUNDERSTOOD

THEY'RE TAKING A LONG TIME.

THEY'RE DEVELOPING A RAPPORT WITH OUR DEALER.

DON'T CALL HIM THAT.

THAT'S WHAT HE IS.

DEALER SOUNDS LIKE A DRUG DEALER.

AS I PREVIOUSLY STATED...

...THAT'S ALMOST LITERALLY *WHAT* HE IS.

HE'S OUR SUPPLIER. YOU WERE THE ONE WHO SAID THAT.

THE SUBTLETIES OF THIS CONVERSATION ARE, LIKE, MAKING ME--

He probably thinks we're, like, twenty-five.

Only twenty-five-year-olds have the amount of money we just gave him.

I couldn't read him.

Was he surprised that we had so much money? Or was he like...not surprised? Which is more offensive?

He had a very weird vibe.

I think that "vibe" is drugs.

Oh, yeah. Definitely drugs.

So, you're saying that he's our dealer and he's on drugs.

What?

RANDY BOWMAN

RIGHT-HANDED

PLAYED ON THE
FOOTBALL TEAM

UNTIL HE BROKE
HIS COLLARBONE

ANYONE
SITTING
HERE?

IS QUICK
WITH WORDS

EVEN QUICKER
WITH HIS HANDS

NO, IT'S
ALL YOURS.

Chew

Chew

Chew

IT'S TEN BUCKS FOR
THE *SUPERLOVE XL* DVD.
I HAVE SOME OTHER
SEXUAL STUFF THAT'S
PRETTY COOL TOO.

AND I ALSO
HAVE JUST PLAIN
ANIME, IF YOU'RE
INTO THAT...

I'M SORRY,
WHAT?

THE ANIME.

I'M
TELLING YOU
THE PRICES
FOR THE
ANIME.

JERRY "KINGPIN" KEPINOWSKI

RIGHT-HANDED

STARTED THE ONE AND ONLY BOWLING ALLEY IN FOREST HILLS SEVENTEEN YEARS AGO

USED TO LOVE BOWLING MORE THAN LIFE ITSELF

HAS A RECURRING DREAM OF BEING A BOWLING BALL STUCK IN A GUTTER

WELL, HELLO THERE! WELCOME TO JERRY KINGPIN'S BOWL-O-RAMA

OVER HERE!

THANK YOU, MR. JERRY KINGPIN, SIR.

WE'RE JUST GONNA--

YEAH, YEAH.

EVERYONE, YOU KNOW BROOKE AND...

...THE OTHER TWO...

HEY, THANKS FOR INVITING US.

WE LOVE BOWLING.

DO WE?

OH, SHOOT. ACTUALLY, I FORGOT MY WALLET AT SCHOOL. DO YOU GUYS MIND PICKING UP THE TAB?

I'LL GET YOU BACK.

I MEAN WE DON'T--

C'MON. YOU GUYS HAVE ALL THAT PORNO MONEY.

IT'S NOT PORN, IT'S ANIME.

WHATEVER THE F@*K THAT IS.

IT'S FINE. WE GOT YOU, JANESSA.

OH, I'M SHORT TOO.

SAME.

SAME.

SAME.

SAME.

A BRIEF HISTORY OF BROOKE'S BIGGEST FEARS

IT'S TIMES LIKE THESE THAT BROOKE MISSES HER MOTHER. NOT BECAUSE THEY'RE WHAT YOU WOULD CALL "CLOSE." QUITE THE OPPOSITE, IN FACT. HOWEVER, FAMILIAL FRICTION IS COMFORTING EVERY NOW AND THEN.

IT BEATS THE CRUSHING SILENCE OF BEING ALONE.

GROWING UP, BROOKE NEVER FELT MORE LOVED THAN WHEN ONE OF HER PARENTS WAS UPSET AT HER. MAYBE IT WAS THE ATTENTION; MAYBE IT WAS THE VOLUME.

BOTH HER MOM AND HER DAD ARE FLUENT IN THE ALMOST-LOST ART OF BASICALLY SCREAMING BUT NOT QUITE.

SHE WORRIES THAT WHEN SHE GETS OLDER, IT WILL AFFECT HER IN A PROFOUND WAY, LIKE BEING TRAPPED IN A CYCLE AND DOING THE SAME THING TO HER KIDS...

THERE'S A SMALL PART OF BROOKE THAT WANTS TO BE STUCK IN SOME DEAD-END TOWN, IN A LOVELESS RELATIONSHIP, OR BEING SCREAMED AT IN FRONT OF TWO KIDS DRESSED IN JACK IN THE BOX UNIFORMS.

LIKE A REALLY SMALL, DARK PART...THAT SHE'S PROBABLY NOT EVEN AWARE OF...

DON'T JUDGE HER; THERE'S LOADS OF WEIRD CONFLICTING, UNHEALTHY FLAWS THAT YOU HAVE, AND WE'RE NOT GIVING YOU THE SIDE-EYE...

BROOKE AND HER MOTHER ONLY SEEM TO TALK WHEN THINGS ARE GOING DOWNHILL. AT MOMENTS OF EXTREME DRAMA.

BUT RIGHT NOW SHE COULD USE HER MOM.

OR AT LEAST SOME ATTENTION.

FROM ANYONE, REALLY...

MELISSA'S POINT OF NO RETURN

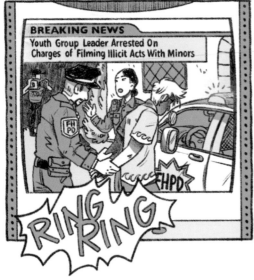

BREAKING NEWS
Youth Group Leader Arrested On
Charges of Filming Illicit Acts With Minors

FHPD

RING RING

HELLO?

OH, HEY.

YEAH, I CAN MEET YOU THERE.

A BRIEF HISTORY OF MELISSA CHO'S RECENT CONFLICTING EMOTIONS

ON HER NINTH BIRTHDAY, MELISSA FOUND A DISPOSABLE CAMERA THAT HER GRANDFATHER HAD LEFT OUT BY MISTAKE. SHE TOOK IT AND KEPT IT UNDER HER BED FOR TWO AND A HALF YEARS. SHE HAD PLANNED TO USE IT ONE DAY. TO CAPTURE SOMETHING SPECIAL.

THESE DAYS, MELISSA FINDS HERSELF FEELING THE CLOSEST THING SHE'S FELT TO HAPPY. OR AT LEAST THAT WAS THE CASE...Y'KNOW...WHEN BROOKE AND KELLY WEREN'T SPEAKING TO EACH OTHER.

MELISSA HAS NEVER FELT LIKE THIS ABOUT SOMEONE. THERE'S A CACOPHONY OF CONFLICTING AND OPPOSING EMOTIONS THAT ARE ALL SWIRLING INSIDE HER. SHE'S NOT SURE WHAT TO DO WITH THEM. SO SHE'S JUST GOING TO IGNORE THEM FOR THE TIME BEING.

SHE'S STARTED PRAYING AT NIGHT FOR ANOTHER MOMENT LIKE THE ONE IN THE WOODS. SHE'S DREADING THE DAY WHEN HER LEG HAIR HAS GROWN OUT, BECAUSE IT WILL BE A DEFINITIVE END TO THE SOLACE SHE FOUND IN THAT QUIET INTIMACY SHE SHARED WITH KELLY.

MELISSA'S BEEN HAVING A RECURRING DAYDREAM ABOUT FINDING THAT OLD DISPOSABLE CAMERA AND TAKING A PICTURE OF KELLY.

MAGGIE, ARE YOU OKAY?

I HAVEN'T EATEN IN, LIKE, THREE DAYS.

MAGGIE...

YOU CAN'T DO THAT.

NOT TO BE INSENSITIVE,

BUT DID YOU SAY YOU HAVEN'T BEEN SELLING THE DVDs?

HALF-STEP ECHOES

WELL, THIS CERTAINLY IS AN INTERESTING DEVELOPMENT.

WHY WAS EVERYTHING YOU SAID A QUESTION?

IT WASN'T--

I JUST-- I DON'T-- I CAN'T--

WAIT, WHERE DID THE MONEY YOU'VE BEEN PUTTING INTO THE WAR CHEST COME FROM?

I'VE BEEN TAKING IT FROM MY MOM'S TIPS...AND I HAD SOME SAVED.

WHAT ARE YOU GONNA DO WITH THEM?

I DON'T WANT ANY PART OF THIS?

I DON'T LIKE DOING THIS?

IT'S WRONG?

STEP

I CAN'T BELIEVE YOU STILL HAVE ALL THIS STUFF.

LOOK.

YOU'VE GOT TO STOP STEALING FROM YOUR MOM. BUT ALSO: THIS COULD JUMP-START EVERYTHING FOR US. WE CAN GET THE BAND BACK TOGETHER.

WHY CAN'T WE GET THE FRIEND-BAND TOGETHER? WHY CAN'T WE JUST HANG OUT AT MY HOUSE? AND BE A BAND OF FRIENDS WHO ARE IN A BAND, THAT ARE FRIENDS?

WHAT?

WHAT DOES THAT EVEN MEAN, MAGGIE?

I DON'T KNOW.

WHAT IF WE TOOK THESE TO JANESSA'S HOUSE PARTY AND SOLD THEM TO THE DUDES THERE?

THAT WOULD BE OUR ULTIMATE REVENGE. WE'D BE MAKING MONEY OFF HER WEIRD PITY INVITE.

YEAH, OR WE'D BE LAUGHED OUT OF THE PARTY.

I MEAN...

YEAH, MAYBE...

I THINK WE SHOULD, LIKE, DO IT.

WHY?

BECAUSE WHAT DO WE HAVE TO LOSE? WE'RE ALREADY THE LAUGHINGSTOCK OF THE WHOLE SCHOOL.

AND WHOSE MONEY WOULD I RATHER TAKE THAN THOSE A#$HOLES'?

MAGGIE?

...

A BRIEF HISTORY OF THE FOREST HILLS BOOTLEG SOCIETY

MAGGIE HILCOT HAS STRUGGLED WITH LONELINESS HER ENTIRE LIFE. IT'S SOMETHING SHE'S GROWN ACCUSTOMED TO. HOWEVER, WHEN SHE MET BROOKE TWO YEARS AGO, EVERYTHING CHANGED.

MAGGIE WAS SITTING BY HERSELF OUTSIDE THE SHIVER ME BURGERS WHEN THIS HAPPENED:

OH, SHUT UP!

YOU'RE TOTALLY A SAILOR JUPITER AND YOU KNOW IT!

OH, S#!T.

I'M SO SORRY ABOUT YOUR FOOD.

WE DON'T HAVE ANY MONEY, BUT...

...WANT TO BE BEST FRIENDS?

FROM THAT MOMENT ON, MAGGIE'S DEVOTION TO HER NEW BEST FRIENDS WAS UNBREAKABLE. EVEN WHEN IT CHALLENGED HER FAITH, HER BETTER JUDGMENT, AND HER GOOD TASTE. IN A NORMAL SCENARIO, THIS STEADFASTNESS WOULD BE A QUALITY TO BE PRAISED. HOWEVER, MAGGIE WOULD SOON COME TO REGRET THE DECISION SHE WAS ABOUT TO MAKE...

OKAY...

LET'S
DO IT.

HEY, DO YOU WANT TO SEE THE NEW MINI COMIC I MADE?

NOT BAD.

Flip Flip Flip

SO, IN OTHER NEWS, I'VE RESTOCKED ON SOME ANIME, IF YOU DUDES ARE INTERESTED? I'VE GOT SOME *DEMON CITY SHINJUKU, SPACE ADVENTURE COBRA,* AND SOME OF THE OTHER MORE HARD-CORE S#!T YOU'LL PROBABLY BE INTO.

OH, ACTUALLY, SCHRETZMAN AND I ARE SAVING UP. WE'RE GONNA TRY AND DO A BIGGER PRINT RUN OF HIS COMICS.

COOL.

LOSERS.

MAGGIE?

OH, HEY, RANDY.

WHAT HAPPENED? YOU HAVEN'T RETURNED MY CALLS?

I'VE JUST GOT SOME STUFF I'VE GOT TO DO.

OKAY, WELL, THERE'S SOME PEOPLE HERE I WANT TO INTRODUCE YOU TO.

I'D LIKE TO, BUT I CAN'T RIGHT NOW.

I'LL CATCH UP WITH YOU LATER, IF THAT'S COOL.

OKAY.

POTENTIAL NEW FRIEND

EVERYTHING YOU'VE EVER WANTED (OR NOT)

POTENTIAL NEW FRIEND

POTENTIAL NEW FRIEND

POTENTIAL NEW FRIEND

OKAY?

I NEED TO BORROW SOME MONEY.

THERE'S SOME COLLEGE KIDS HERE WITH A KEG, AND IT'S WAY MORE EXPENSIVE THAN THEY TOLD US.

I'LL PAY YOU BACK, I PROMISE.

I DON'T HAVE ANY MONEY.

I JUST SAW YOU MAKE MONEY OFF THAT KID. MAYBE WE CAN POOL OUR MONEY?

I MEAN...

I'M SORRY ABOUT THE STUFF AT THE BOWLING ALLEY. IT WAS SUPPOSED TO BE FUNNY...

I JUST...

SOMETIMES YOU DO THINGS... AND YOU'RE NOT SURE WHY...

SOMETIMES IT'S HARD...

...TO MAKE THINGS STOP...

PLEASE, I NEED HELP.

...

FINE.

RUSTLE

RUSTLE

RUSTLE

MELISSA AND KELLY'S FIRST KISS

FOREST HILLS, CA

POPULATION 8,992

FOUNDED IN 1881

HENRY CLAYTON HARDWOOD'S GRAVE WAS RECENTLY VANDALIZED

CATHERINE HOLLINGS'S IS IN THE PROCESS OF SELLING HER HOME

SHE PLANS ON MOVING TO BLITHE, ARIZONA. SHE HAS SOME FAMILY THERE

THE MEMORIES HERE ARE OVERWHELMING

TO SAY NOTHING OF THE CASSEROLES

DESPITE THE UBIQUITY OF THIS AFFORDABLE RETAIL CHAIN, THIS PARTICULAR CHEAP-O FOOTBOATS IS NOT DOING VERY WELL

THEY'RE IN THE PROCESS OF CLOSING. SOON THIS LOCATION WILL BECOME A GET YO'GURT

Chapter: 8

ENTROPY

IN THIS MOMENT...

HANK FEELS ALMOST FINE.

FOR ONCE.

SSLLUUUPPP

CRASH

BOOOM

PUSH

WELL, I'VE SEEN ENOUGH. THANK YOU, LADIES. PRINCIPAL ARDEN AND I WILL NEED TO SPEAK WITH YOUR PARENTS.

THIS IS PROBABLY GOING TO BE THE LAST TIME WE ALL TALK TO EACH OTHER.

MAGGIE HILCOT

MELISSA CHO

RIGHT-HANDED

WISHES HER MOM HAD BEEN THERE TO SCOLD HER WITH THE OTHER GIRLS

DATED KELLY FOR THREE MONTHS, THEN GOT TIRED OF NOT HAVING THE EXCITEMENT OF A SECRET TRYST

HER INTEREST IN THE CIRCUS IS WANING, JUST SLIGHTLY...

GOES TO YOUTH GROUP REGULARLY NOW

STILL SECRETLY LIKES ANIME

KELLY NAHAS

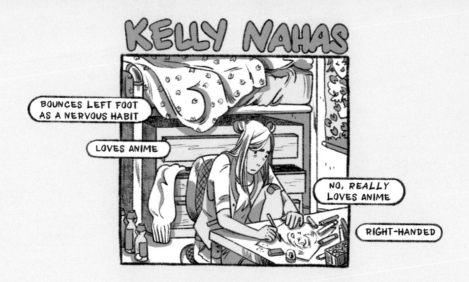

BOUNCES LEFT FOOT AS A NERVOUS HABIT

LOVES ANIME

NO, REALLY LOVES ANIME

RIGHT-HANDED

HAS A RECURRING DREAM OF MOVING TO JAPAN

WANTS TO WORK IN THE ANIME INDUSTRY

DOESN'T HAVE THE SKILL OR WORK ETHIC TO SUCCEED

DEEP DOWN SHE KNOWS THIS

BUT SHE STILL TRIES, ANYWAY...

BROOKE IMAFIDON

LIVES WITH HER MOM IN THE BAY AREA

GOES TO A PUBLIC SCHOOL

HAS A FEW FRIENDS

TURNED HER THREE-PAGE PAPER ON TOTALITARIANISM IN EARLY

HAS A NEW GIRLFRIEND...

MAYBE...

DATING IS COMPLICATED...

SOMETIMES SHE GETS IN FIGHTS WITH HER MOM...

SOMETIMES...

BROOKE SHOULD BE HAPPY...

BUT SHE JUST ISN'T

BURN TO MEDIA - {DISC}

BURN OPTIONS | BURN PROGESS

BURN SPEED: `16X(22, 160 KB/S)`   NUMBER OF COPIES `1`

BURN METHOD

DISC AT ONCE

SESSION AT ONCE

BURN OPTIONS

☑ USE BUFFER PROTECTION

☐ SIMULATE BURNING PROCESS

☐ MODE2XA INSTEAD OF MODE 1

☐ CACHE COMPILATION BEFORE BURNING

☐ SHUTDOWN COMPUTER AFTER COMPLETION

☐ FINALIZE DISC

☑ EJECT DISC AFTER BURNING

☐ VERIFY DATA AFTER BURNING

[BURN DISC]   [CANCEL]

EVOLVE OR DIE

WELL, YOU'VE FINISHED OUR BOOK. Thank you. From the bottom of my heart, thank you. You don't know what it means to me that our book has found you. Nicole and I have been working on it for longer than I care to remember, and harder than I want to admit. There have been literal years of labor put into the pages that you've just read. Hopefully it shows. I'm exceedingly proud of the work Nicole and I have produced in this volume. I think it's a pretty accurate reflection of who we are and what we believe.

And that right there is the end goal.

I believe different art forms have different aims. For me, I think the goal of creating comics is to produce a record of who I am, who I was, or who I hope to be. And that's the thing with art—and being a human—you're always evolving. So, it's important to have a record so you can remind yourself where you've come from.

As I sit here, in my apartment, typing this essay, I find myself thinking about how much my perspective on the work has shifted and changed over time. And how, with any luck, it will be a book that people can have a relationship with and make their own drifting connections to.

All good art evolves. Both in a literal sense and metaphorical. When you first start to build an idea that will eventually become a book, you have this vision of what it will be. It's a hazy view. But there's something that pushes you forward it. And as you refine it and hone it ... it evolves.

Then, after you've made it, the work is theoretically inert, but the way you think about it evolves as you come to terms with its flaws or its shortcomings. And then it goes out into the world ... and people find a sense of connection to it ... and it changes again.

At this point, *Forest Hills Bootleg Society* has evolved so many times that I'm a little reticent to tell you what we initially set out to do. I don't know that it matches what we have now.

For Nicole and me, that's what comics are. Or at least that's what they aspire to be: evolutionary reflections of a collective dream we've had. Not documents or records of actual happenings, but a shimmering doppelganger comprised of our joint hallucination.

I find it somewhat sad to think about the biographies of projects. About how many books go unpublished and about the struggle and length of time it takes to finally see your work put out into the world.

But that's part of the process of creating. If it were easy, everyone would do it and it wouldn't mean anything. The inherent difficulty involved in producing the close to 230 pages you've just read are a testament to that. They're a witness to the commitment that Nicole and I have to the greatest artistic medium of all time: comics.

When we started talking about the book that would eventually become *Forest Hills Bootleg Society*, we talked a lot about our respective high school experiences, our maturing, and our formative moments. When I was in high school, I ended up buying bootleg anime from a smelly kid named Max, burned onto a DVD. I remember secreting it away and using a portable DVD player to watch it late into the night. There's something about finding your own emotional pocket dimension at that age that has a magic and a safety to it that doesn't exist at almost any other point in life. That feeling became the root emotion and guiding light for the process of creating this book. I wanted to try to replicate that tangibly interior feeling of finding something that's exclusively yours.

To be frank, I wanted our book to function like that for someone else. To be their secret. To be their dog-eared friend that they repeatedly escaped into when the world proved too tough.

My experience discovering bootleg DVDs led me to a simple and yet profound realization. Art is something that can save you. It can be used as a standard for your hopes, dreams, and beliefs. For some people, that art can become a trap. It can devour your identity. It can become an overwhelming and crushing weight. Or it can be a conduit to making friends and developing lifelong relationships. It all depends on how you use the power that art can give us all.

Nicole and I wanted to create something that both reflected our experiences and worked as a call to arms. A rallying cry for people who needed it. A beam of light in the darkness that said, "You're not alone.... And also: anime is pretty cool, I guess."

We have worked on quite a few projects together. If you liked this book, please check out our other books *F**k Off Squad* and *Everyone Is Tulip*. We approach each of our books with a unique vision or goal. We want to make work that transcends the boundaries of the page, and hopefully really connects with people. We think of ourselves as a band. Only we don't make music. We make comics. Comics that can, for the right person, save their life.

Our ultimate goal was to create the book that, had we found it in high school, would have changed our lives. It's not really up to us to say if that's happened or not, but that was the mission. We set out to tell a story that had a tangible sense of vulnerability and was about how hard it can be to attempt to grow and change. And how sometimes that growth comes in unexpected or less-than-healthy ways. We wanted to explore the traumas of infidelity and organized religion. And how the former feels like it will follow you for the rest of your days, while, in reality, it's the latter that will more often than not prove inescapable.

Just like the characters in our book try and fail and stumble forward into adulthood, I think *Forest Hills Bootleg Society* is a perfect sense-memory document of Nicole's and my personal evolution. I look at the pages, and I can immediately remember where we were when we had specific ideas or conversations. I can remember which subplots we deleted or altered. But that's my personal connection to the work—and now the work has found you. And you will create your own history and connection with it. If we've done our jobs right, this book will play a role in your personal evolution... which is all any artist can hope for.

YOUR FRIEND,
DAVEY
LOS ANGELES, 2022

An imprint of Simon & Schuster Children's Publishing Division
1230 Avenue of the Americas, New York, New York 10020
For information about special discounts for bulk purchases, please contact Simon & Schuster Special Sales at 1-866-506-1949 or business@simonandschuster.com.
The Simon & Schuster Speakers Bureau can bring authors to your live event. For more information or to book an event, contact the Simon & Schuster Speakers Bureau at 1-866-248-3049 or visit our website at www.simonspeakers.com.
The illustrations for this book were rendered digitally.
Manufactured in China
First Edition
1 2 3 4 5 6 7 8 9 10
CIP data for this book is available from the Library of Congress.
ISBN 9781534469488 (pbk)
ISBN 9781534469495 (hc)
ISBN 9781534469501 (ebook)